Welcome to Sparklegrove

Read more
UNICORN DIARIES
books!

Unicorn Diaries

Welcome to Sparklegrove

Rebecca Elliott

BRANCHES

SCHOLASTIC INC.

Dedicated to all those who have had
to find new homes. May they always
be welcomed. XX —R.E.

Special thanks to Clare Wilson
for her contributions to this book.

Library of Congress Cataloging-in-Publication Data

Names: Elliott, Rebecca, author, illustrator.
Title: Welcome to sparklegrove / Rebecca Elliott.
Description: First edition. | New York : Branches/Scholastic, Inc., 2023. |
Series: Unicorn diaries ; 8 | Audience: Ages 5–7. | Audience: Grades K–2. |
Summary: Bo Tinseltail and friends welcome a jackalope family
to Sparklegrove Forest, and when they learn the family is being chased by
centaurs everyone bands together to help the jackalopes live in peace.
Identifiers: LCCN 2022010608 (print) | ISBN 9781338745658 (paperback) |
ISBN 9781338745665 (library binding) |
Subjects: CYAC: Unicorns—Fiction. | Mythical animals—Fiction. | Bullies
and bullying—Fiction. | Helpfulness—Fiction. | Diaries—Fiction. |
BISAC: JUVENILE FICTION / Readers / Chapter Books | JUVENILE FICTION /
Animals / Dragons, Unicorns & Mythical
Classification: LCC PZ7.E45812 We 2023 (print) | DDC [Fic]—dc23
LC record available at https://lccn.loc.gov/2022010608

ISBN 978-1-338-74566-5 (hardcover) / ISBN 978-1-338-74565-8 (paperback)

10 9 8 7 6 5 4 3 2 1   23 24 25 26 27

Printed in China   62
First edition, April 2023

Edited by Katie Carella
Book design by Marissa Asuncion

Table of Contents

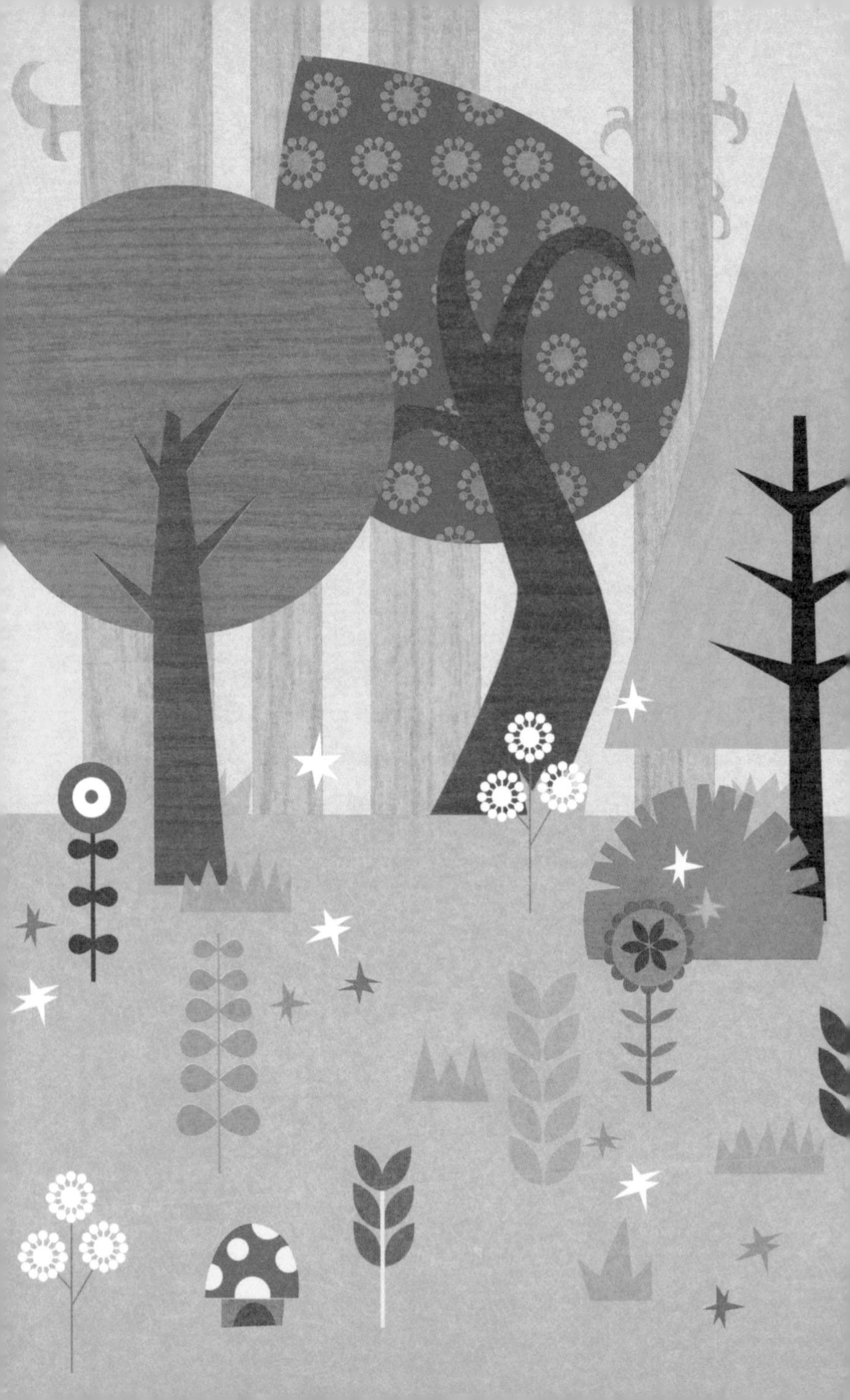

1

A New Family!

Hello there, Diary! It's your favorite unicorn again — Rainbow Tinseltail. You can call me Bo.

My friends and I are super excited because a family of JACKALOPES arrived at our forest last night! I can't wait to meet them!

Rainbow Falls

Gnome
Tunnels

Troll
Caves

Glimmer
Glade

Sparklegrove School
for Unicorns

Dragon
Nests

Budbloom
Meadow

Snowbelle Mountain

Unipods

Fairy Village

Goldie's Cave

Twinkleplop Lagoon

Goblin Castle

Lots of magical creatures live here, but there have never been any jackalopes!

Here's what I know about jackalopes:

They hop like rabbits, but they are bigger than rabbits.

They have big ears and great hearing.

They eat carrots.

Sadly, mean creatures hunt them for their special antlers.

Unicorns are pretty interesting, too. Here's some information about us:

Horn
Glows so we can see in the dark.

Ears
Bob up and down when we hear music!

Tail
Swishing it makes our powers work. (It's also good for batting away flies!)

Mouth
We can neigh like a horse, but we choose not to.

Want to learn more cool unicorn facts?

Some unicorns can fly. A feather from a flying unicorn's wing can power a witch's broomstick!

We sleep on small floating clouds.

We don't have parents. Our friends are our family!

We exercise our tails to keep them good at swishing.

Me and my friends go to Sparklegrove School for Unicorns (S.S.U.). We live and sleep there – in **UNIPODS**.

My friends all have different Unicorn Powers. Because I'm a Wish Unicorn, I can grant one wish every week.

This is my BEST friend, Sunny Huckleberry. He is a Crystal-Clear Unicorn, which means he can turn invisible!

Here are my other S.S.U. pals, with their powers.

Nutmeg Silvertips

Flying Unicorn

Scarlett Sugarlumps

Thingamabob Unicorn

Jed Glitterock

Weather Unicorn

Monty Dumpling

Size-Changer Unicorn

Piper Forestine

Healer Unicorn

Mr. Rumptwinkle

our teacher

Shape-Shifter Unicorn

At school, we learn **GLITTERRIFIC** stuff, like:

GLITTEROLOGY
(The Science of Glitter)

CLEANING AND TIDYING

MAGICAL MINDFULNESS

HAIR-OBICS
(Tail Exercising)

Every week, we also learn or try to do something new. When we succeed, we get a special unicorn patch that we sew onto our patch blankets.

I wonder which patch we'll work toward this week. I hope it has something to do with the new jackalope family! Good night, Diary!

Welcome Party

At breakfast, we were all talking about the new family moving into the forest.

I heard they arrived at the castle last night!

Exciting! I can't wait to meet a jackalope!

I wonder how big their antlers are!

I wonder how high they can hop!

It must be scary moving to a new place.

I wonder why they left their old place.

We should throw them a welcome party!

★ 13 ★

Just then, Mr. Rumptwinkle joined us.

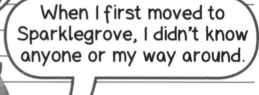

We were all a bit shocked. We'd thought Mr. Rumptwinkle had always lived here!

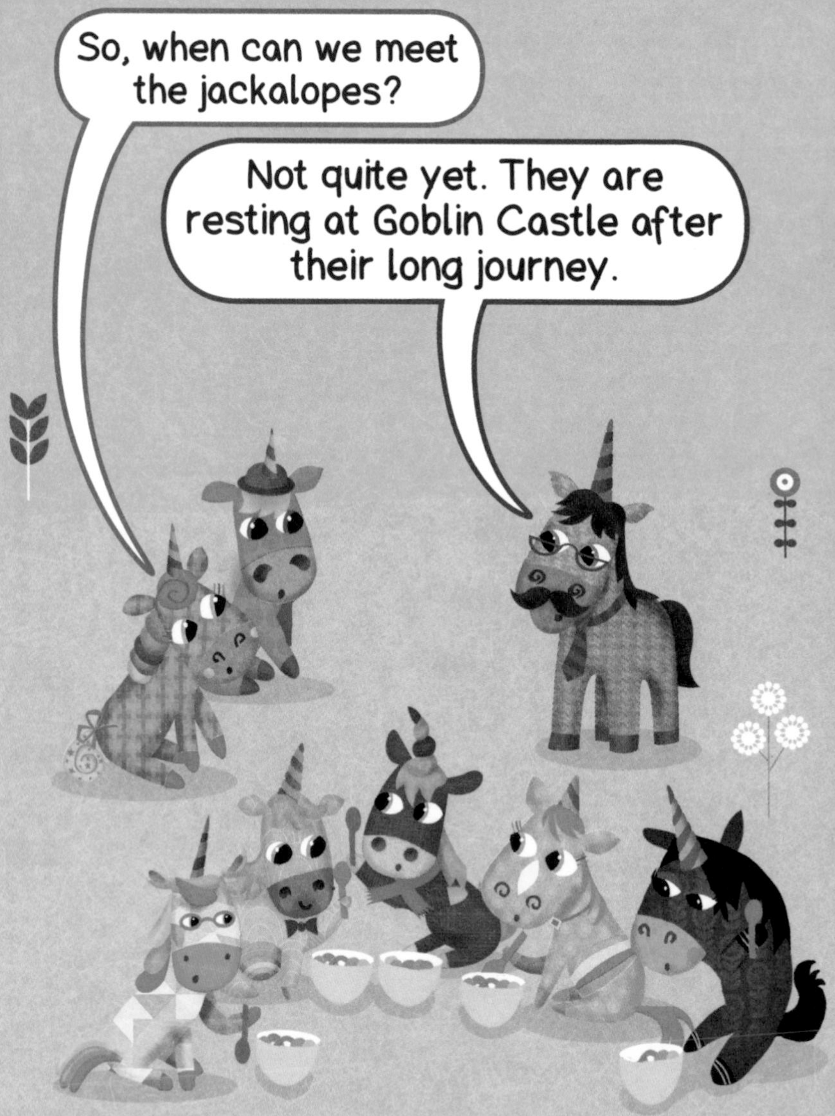
So, when can we meet the jackalopes?
Not quite yet. They are resting at Goblin Castle after their long journey.

We started party planning and came up with the following list. What do you think, Diary?

<u>Welcome Party To-Do List:</u>

- Make a banner

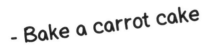

- Bake a carrot cake

- Make a gift:
  Draw a map of
  Sparklegrove
  Forest!

We're going to make those jackalopes feel so welcome!

Sunny, Nutmeg, Monty, and I made the welcome banner, which of course involved a lot of glitter.

This looks great! Where shall we hang it?

We should put it near the castle now rather than waiting until the party. That way, it'll be the first thing the jackalopes see when they come out of the castle!

We trotted to the castle.

Nutmeg and Monty hung the banner high up in the trees.

When we got home, we checked on Piper, Scarlett, and Jed. They had made a rainbow-colored carrot cake.

We talked about the extra guards outside the castle.

We all threw frosting at one another. It was the yummiest battle ever! Then we had fun tidying up . . .

With our bellies full of frosting, we went to bed excited to meet the jackalopes!

3

Meeting a Unicorn

Tuesday

Today we started drawing a big map of Sparklegrove Forest.

Don't forget Rainbow Falls!

Then two guards showed up. They looked very serious and were talking with Mr. Rumptwinkle.

When the guards left, we saw that Mr. Rumptwinkle was holding a royal invitation!

Unicorns, I've been invited to speak privately with Queen Juniper.

Why?

Sometimes she asks me for advice.

You <u>are</u> very wise.

Well, I don't know about that. But thank you!

Then he left.

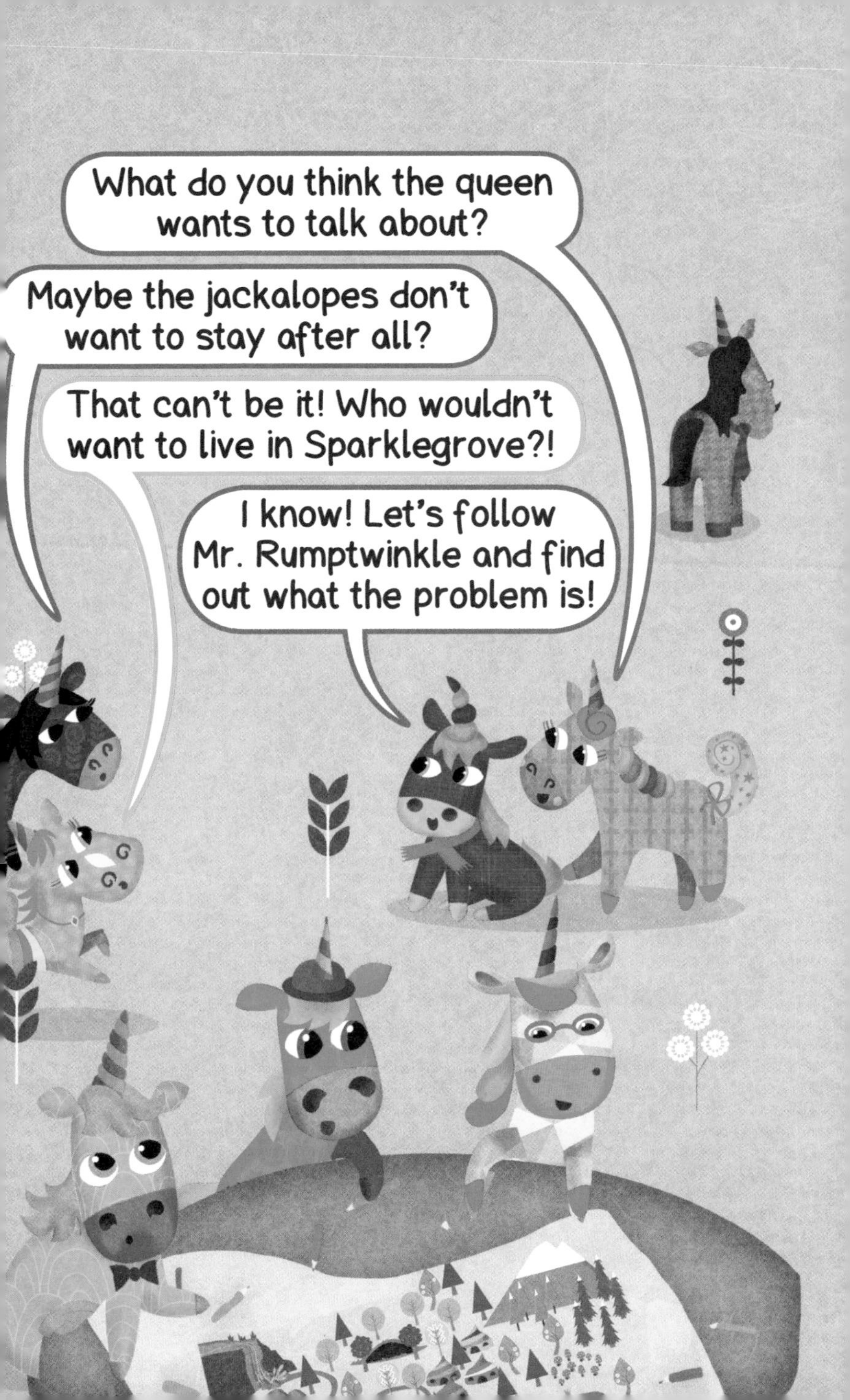
What do you think the queen wants to talk about?
Maybe the jackalopes don't want to stay after all?
That can't be it! Who wouldn't want to live in Sparklegrove?!
I know! Let's follow Mr. Rumptwinkle and find out what the problem is!

At the castle, there were still lots of guards.

Greta was dragging three huge sacks of carrots!

Greta told the guards we were there on important royal business, so they let us in.

But he couldn't understand me!

In the castle gardens, we saw two confused-looking guards.

Hello, guards! Where are the jackalopes?

Well, the jackalope parents are inside talking with the queen.

And the little one is out here somewhere . . . He keeps hiding from us!

Oh. I see.

A young jackalope hopped out from behind a tree!

We got to know Bounder while Greta went to get picnic supplies. What was great was that Bounder was as excited to meet us as we were to meet him!

Hi, Bounder! It's very nice to meet you!

I've always wanted to meet a <u>unicorn</u>!

Do you neigh?

No! We're not horses!

I can jump high – look!

Wow! That's really high!

I know! I've got skills! But unicorns have magical powers, right?! Show me!

Piper and I made our horns glow and told him about our Unicorn Powers.

Then Nutmeg flew.

Scarlett magicked up a toy unicorn for Bounder.

Monty went
super small.

Jed made it
snow.

And Sunny turned invisible, apart
from his bottom.

Ha ha! You are
all AMAZING!

Greta came back with a delicious picnic!

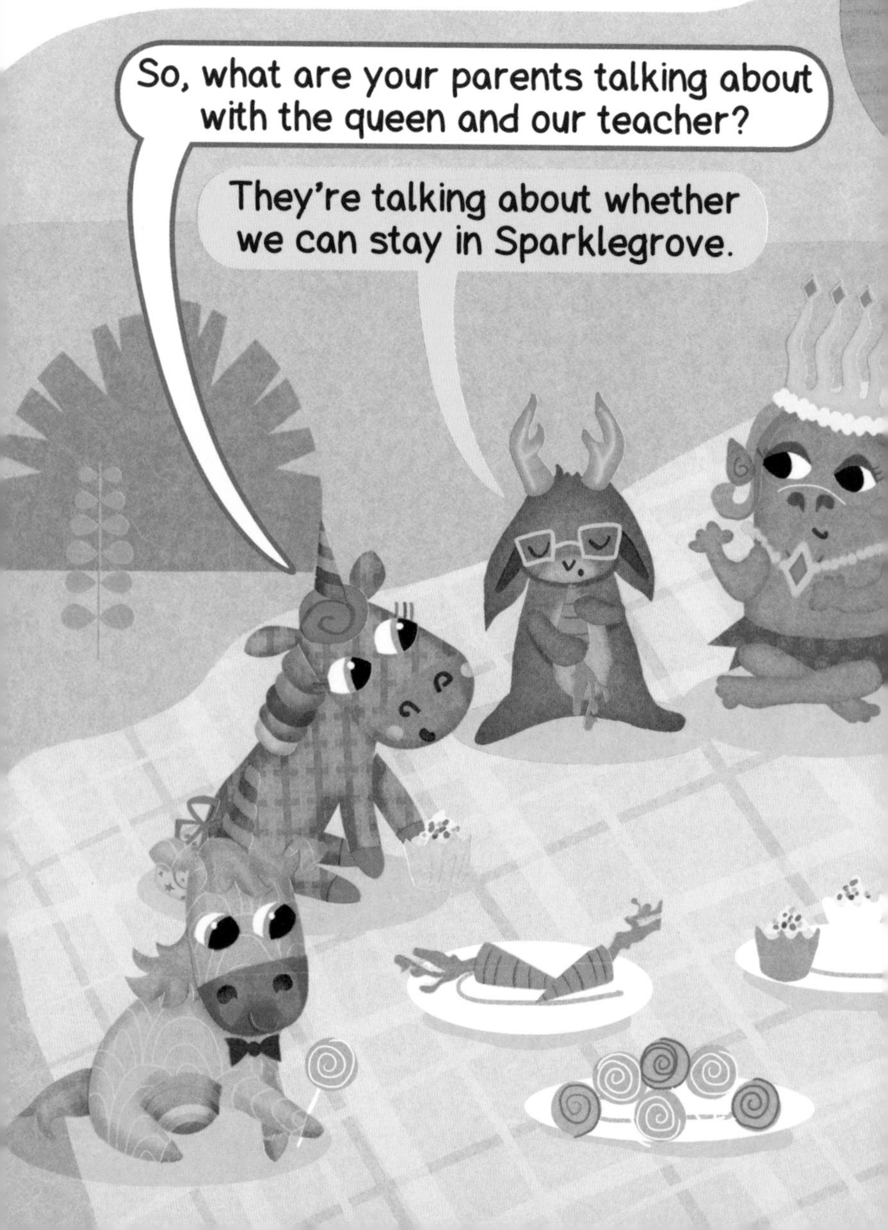
So, what are your parents talking about with the queen and our teacher?
They're talking about whether we can stay in Sparklegrove.

Poor Bounder looked VERY sad, so we didn't keep asking him questions. But we were all wondering: Why might the jackalopes have to leave?

Back at the **UNIPODS**, we waited for Mr. Rumptwinkle. When he finally got home, we asked him lots of questions.

But Mr. Rumptwinkle couldn't tell us much.

Oh Diary. We love little Bounder!
I really hope he can stay!

4

Bounding About

At breakfast today, we had only one thing to talk about: the jackalope family!

I wish we knew why they might have to leave.

There must be good reasons.

Well, maybe we can't welcome the <u>whole</u> family to Sparklegrove yet, but we can welcome Bounder!

You're right, Bo! Let's show him around the forest!

Yes! Today might be our only chance.

So we all trotted to the castle.

When we arrived, we talked to the guards.

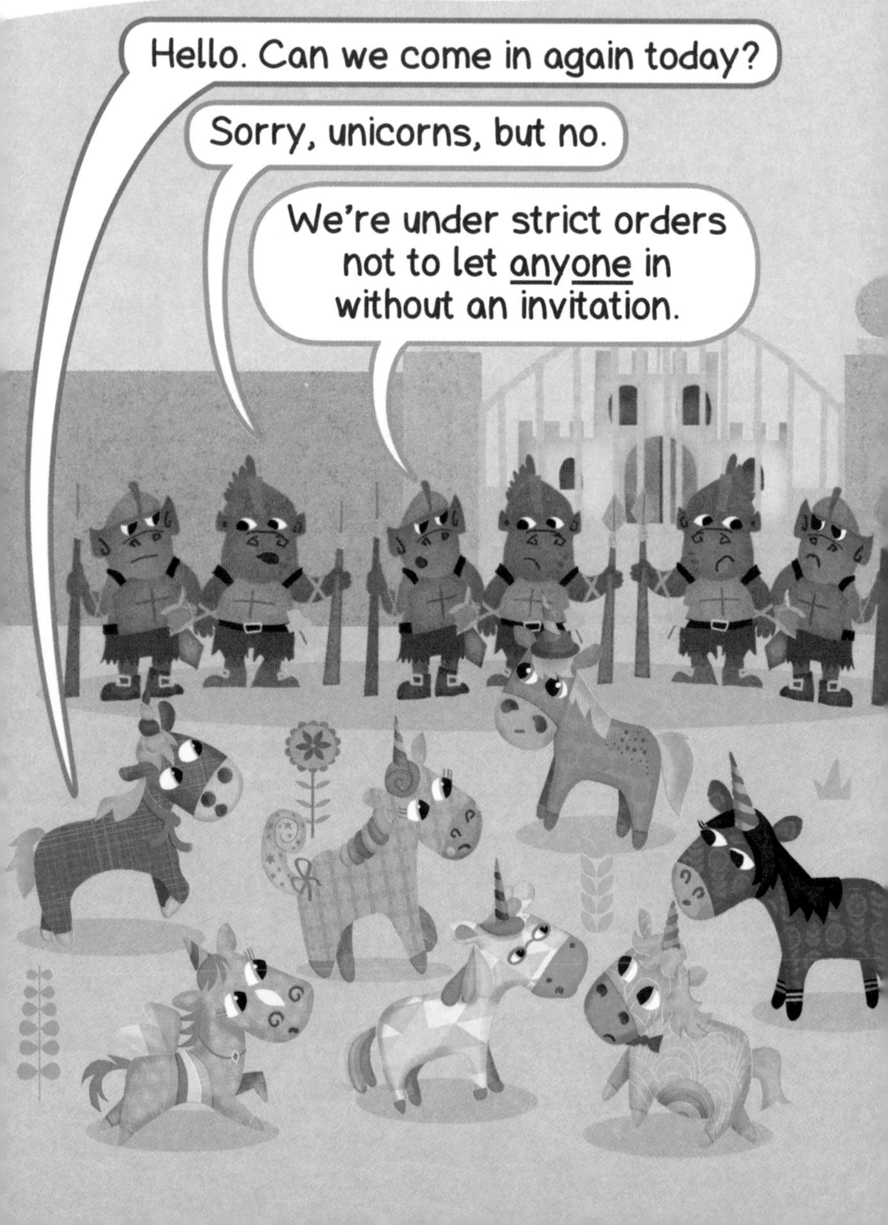
Hello. Can we come in again today?
Sorry, unicorns, but no.
We're under strict orders not to let anyone in without an invitation.

We hid behind a bush to brainstorm a new plan. That's when we saw Bounder, hopping high into the air behind the castle wall.

If only there were a way for us to talk to him.

That's it! I know what to do!

First, Sunny made himself invisible.

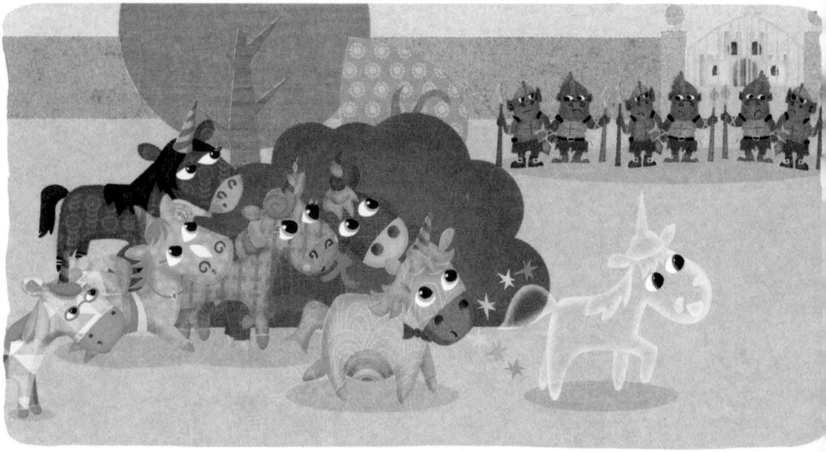

Next, Sunny snuck up to the wall and whispered to Bounder.

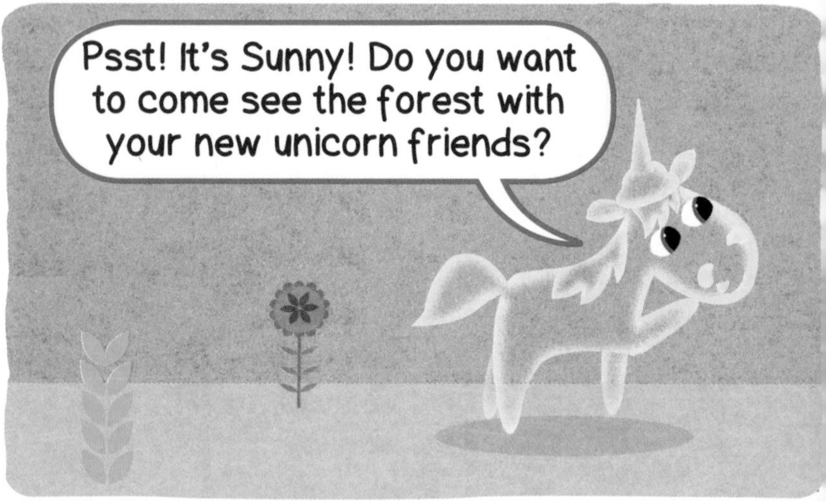
Psst! It's Sunny! Do you want to come see the forest with your new unicorn friends?

Sunny waited . . . We all hoped our lessons on magical creatures had been right — that jackalopes have great hearing. Then Sunny heard a reply!

Then Bounder did a HUGE leap and landed right next to us!

We had fun giving Bounder a tour of the forest.

We ran around in Budbloom Meadow.

We swam in Rainbow Falls.

And Bounder met lots of magical creatures who live here.

Bounder loved our tour. And everyone he met loved him!

Back at our **UNIPODS**, Scarlett magicked up carrot cupcakes. Bounder made us laugh when he stuck two on his antlers to "save for later."

We'd better head back before anyone starts worrying about you.

Outside the castle, Bounder suddenly looked sad.

Bounder, what's wrong?

I really want to stay in Sparklegrove.

Well, maybe we can help! __Why__ might you have to leave?

That's when Bounder told us his story . . .

My family and I had to run away from our old forest because we were being hunted by some mean centaurs.

Your queen wants to protect my family, but she and my parents are worried that if we stay, those centaurs will track us down. Then everyone in Sparklegrove will be in danger.

Bounder said good-bye and jumped
back into the castle gardens.

We all went to bed feeling worried.

Oh, Sunny, I really want the jackalopes to stay. But I am scared of those centaurs coming here.

I know. Hopefully, we'll find out more from Mr. Rumptwinkle in the morning.

It took me a long time to fall asleep.

5
Midnight at Goblin Castle

Thursday

This morning, we talked to Mr. Rumptwinkle.

We've heard that some centaurs are after the jackalope family!

How did you hear that?

We told him about meeting Bounder and giving him a tour of the forest.

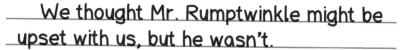

We thought Mr. Rumptwinkle might be upset with us, but he wasn't.

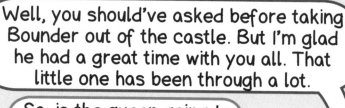

Well, you should've asked before taking Bounder out of the castle. But I'm glad he had a great time with you all. That little one has been through a lot.

So, is the queen going to let the jackalopes stay?

We want them to stay, but I'm scared of the centaurs.

Me too.

I can understand your worries, unicorns. But let me share what happened to me . . .

When I first came here, it was because the creatures in the forest I came from weren't very nice to me. They said I wasn't a <u>real</u> unicorn because I was a shape-shifter.

Sparklegrove forest

Oh, that's awful.

Yes. But everyone here made me feel at home. Sparklegrove is a special place — not because of its magic, but because it welcomes and takes care of <u>everyone</u>.

This made us stop and think. Then Nutmeg said what we were all thinking.

Then Mr. Rumptwinkle frowned.

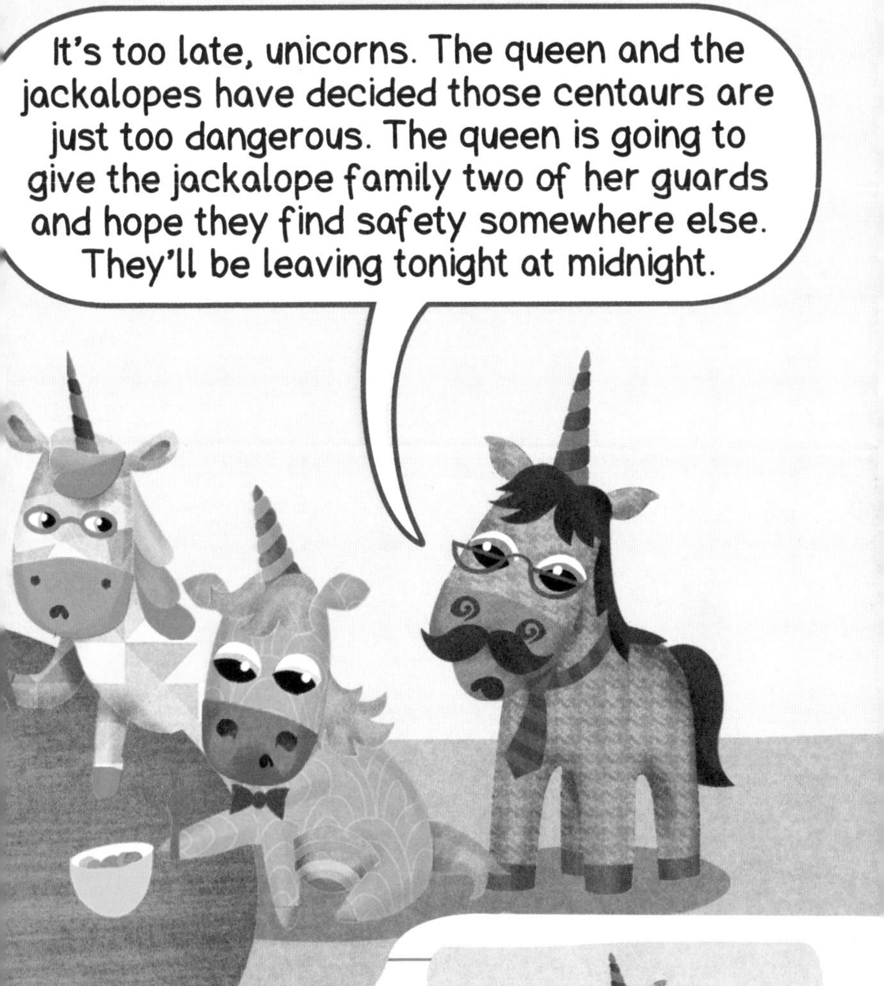
It's too late, unicorns. The queen and the jackalopes have decided those centaurs are just too dangerous. The queen is going to give the jackalope family two of her guards and hope they find safety somewhere else. They'll be leaving tonight at midnight.

Mr. Rumptwinkle trotted off sadly.

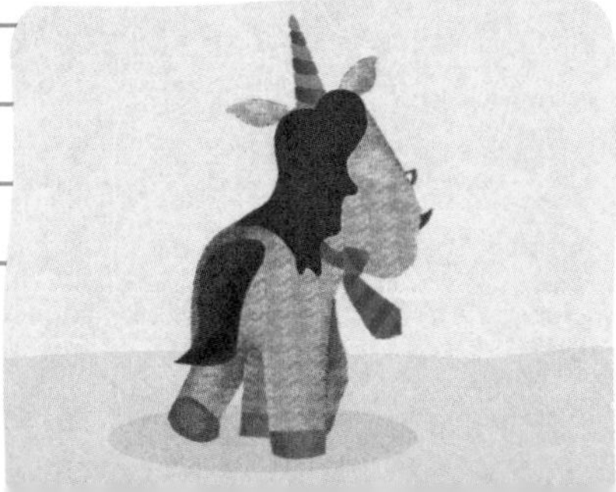

There must be something we can do!

Even if our forest friends knew about the dangerous centaurs, I don't think they'd want the jackalope family to leave — especially now that so many of them have met Bounder!

Let's go talk with them!

We went to see everyone Bounder had met yesterday.

We told them about the centaurs and about the jackalopes leaving tonight.

This is so unfair!

That poor little jackalope and his family!

The jackalopes must stay in Sparklegrove!

Sparklegrove IS a very special place. Even though those centaurs are scary, everyone wanted the jackalopes to stay. Even the trolls!

So, together, we made a plan.

Just before midnight, the castle gates opened for the jackalopes to leave. They, the queen, and Mr. Rumptwinkle were shocked to see us all there!

Then Queen Juniper smiled and spoke to the jackalopes.

Suddenly, we heard hooves galloping toward the castle. Then — DISASTER! Two centaurs turned up!

6
And Don't Come Back!

Friday

We were all super scared as the mean centaurs pointed arrows at us.

We only want the jackalopes. Hand them over!

Please don't hurt anyone. We will go with you.

PLEASE STAY! Sparklegrove Welcomes you!

No, wait!

Before the centaurs knew what was happening, we had all formed a wall in front of the jackalopes.

These jackalopes are part of our Sparklegrove family. So you will have to go through us to get to them!

We didn't want to hurt the centaurs, but we did want to frighten them. So the fairies fired arrows and the trolls threw rocks <u>near</u> them. The dragons breathed fire into the air, too.

GO AWAY!

Now the centaurs were the ones who looked scared!

When the centaurs left, everyone cheered! Bounder gave me a big hug!

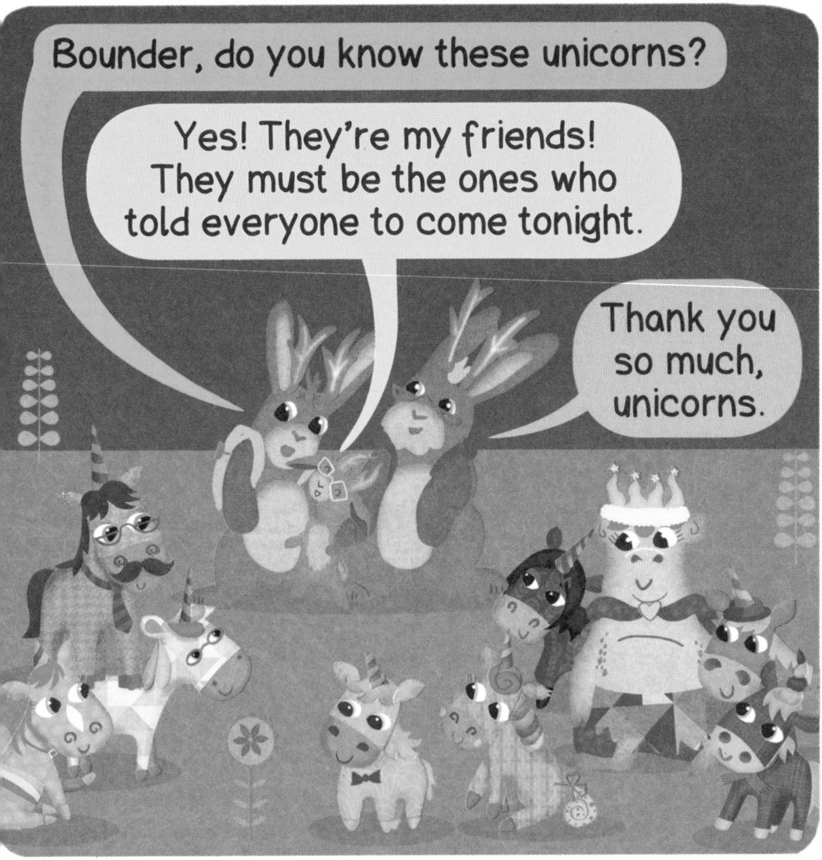
Bounder, do you know these unicorns?
Yes! They're my friends! They must be the ones who told everyone to come tonight.
Thank you so much, unicorns.

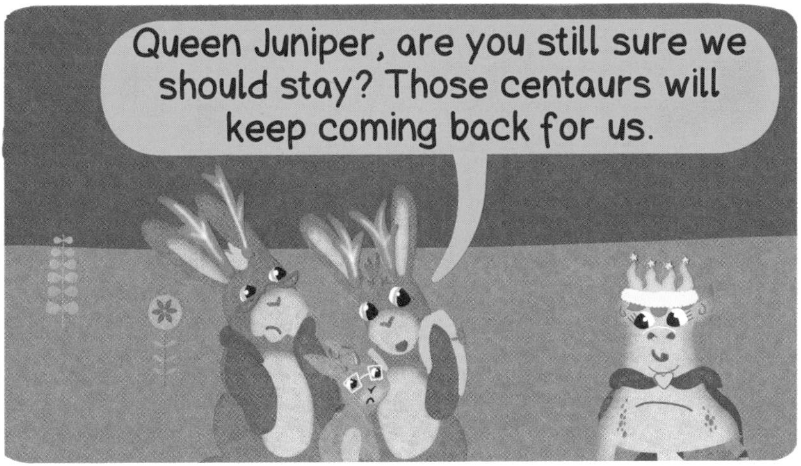
Queen Juniper, are you still sure we should stay? Those centaurs will keep coming back for us.

Then Bounder said JUST the right thing!

I wish those mean centaurs could never set hoof in Sparklegrove Forest again!

You <u>wish</u>? Then your wish is granted!

Wow! So we can stay and everyone will be safe?!

Yes, this is your home now!

I can't wait to REALLY celebrate at the welcome party later today!

7

Welcome to the Family

The jackalope family loved the map we made them! They started to make their burrow in Budbloom Meadow.

We're planting a carrot patch for you!

Thank you!

Yummy!

The welcome party was **SPARKLETASTIC** fun! We ate carrot cake and danced!

HOME OF THE JACKALOPES

Then Mr. Rumptwinkle gave us our WELCOME patches.

Thank you for reminding all of us that Sparklegrove is one big family and we are always there for each other.

So this week, our Sparklegrove
family got even bigger and happier!

See you next time, Diary!

Rebecca Elliott may not have a magical horn or sneeze glitter, but she's still a lot like a unicorn. Rebecca always tries to have a positive attitude, she likes to laugh a lot, and she lives with some great creatures — her noisy-yet-charming children, her lovable but naughty dog, Frida, and a big, lazy cat named Bernard. She gets to hang out with these fun characters and write stories for a living, so she thinks her life is pretty magical!

Rebecca is the author of several picture books, the young adult novel PRETTY FUNNY FOR A GIRL, the Unicorn Diaries early chapter book series, and the *New York Times*–bestselling Owl Diaries series.

Unicorn Diaries

How much do you know about Welcome to Sparklegrove?

Mr. Rumptwinkle did not always live in Sparklegrove Forest. Why did he leave the forest he lived in before?

Moving to a new place can be scary. Have you ever moved? If so, how did you feel about it? If not, how do you think it would feel to make your home in a new place?

The jackalope family is being chased by mean centaurs. Why is this group of centaurs chasing them? Reread page 4.

The unicorns throw the jackalope family a welcome party. If you threw a welcome party, what kind of cake and decorations would you make? Draw what your party would look like!

The unicorns make a map of Sparklegrove for the jackalope family. Make a map of your neighborhood. Then give it to a friend!